Why can't I walk upside-down?

Written by Julie Penn
Illustrated by Abdi

Collins

Who and what is in this book?

Listen and say

Sue

Download the audio at www.collins.co.uk/839788

spiders

Matt

Matt is playing a game.
He says, "I can walk upside-down!"

4

Sue says, "People can't walk upside-down!"

Matt says, "But spiders can! How?"

Spiders have hair on their legs.

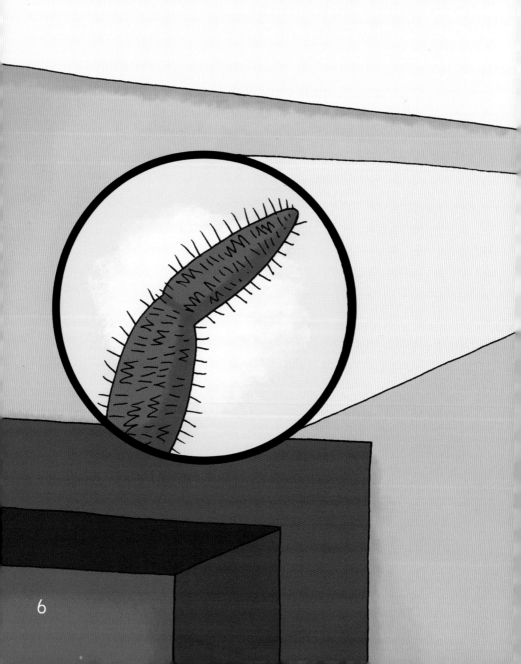

The hair here is sticky. It helps the spider to climb.

Some spiders are big and some
are small.

Spiders have eight legs.

Look! This spider has eight eyes, too.

Lots of spiders live in our gardens.

Some spiders live in our houses, too!

Many spiders are black or brown, but some have lots of colours.

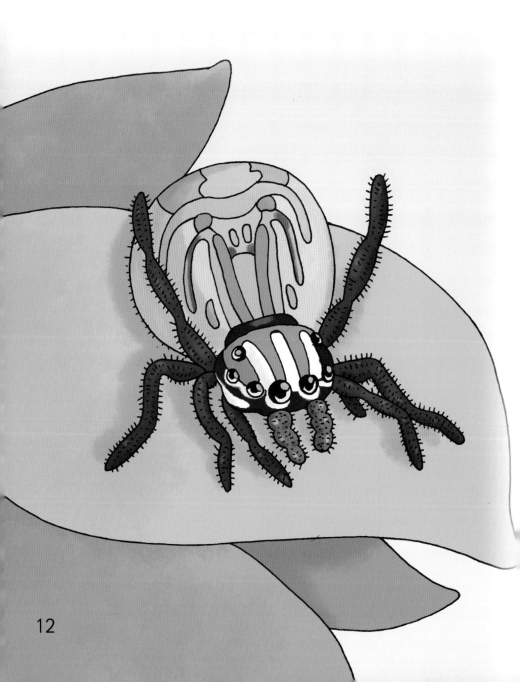

Some spiders can change their colours.
Can you see the spider on this flower?

Spiders can make silk. They use the silk for lots of things.

These spiders are using the silk
to climb.

Look! It's a ball of silk. There are spider eggs in the ball.

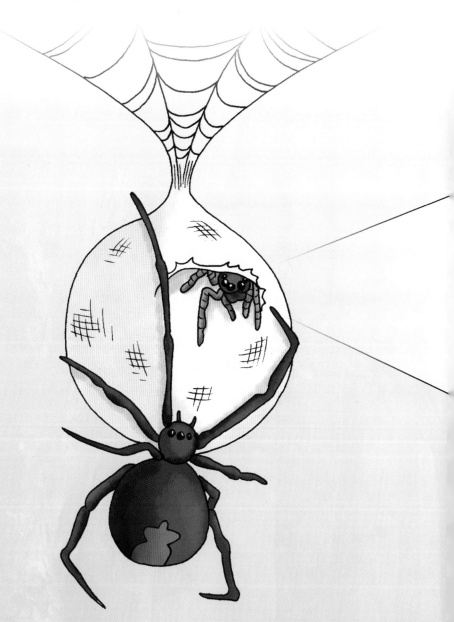

The baby spiders can use their silk to fly.

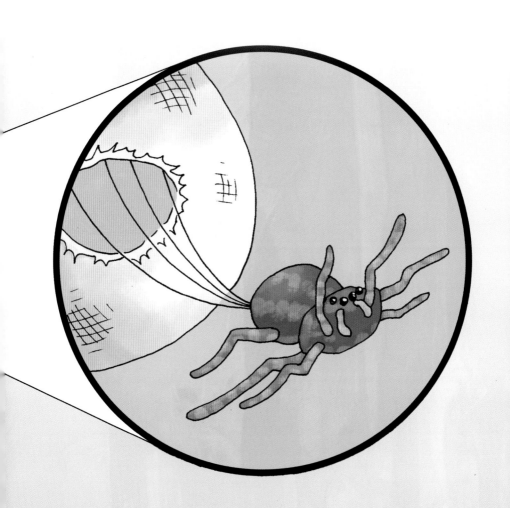

This spider is making a web.
The silk is sticky.

The spider catches food in the web.

Matt says, "Look, Sue. I'm a spider in a web!"

Sue says, "Oh yes. Now you *can* walk upside-down!"

Picture dictionary

Listen and repeat 🎧 ③

change

climb

eyes

legs

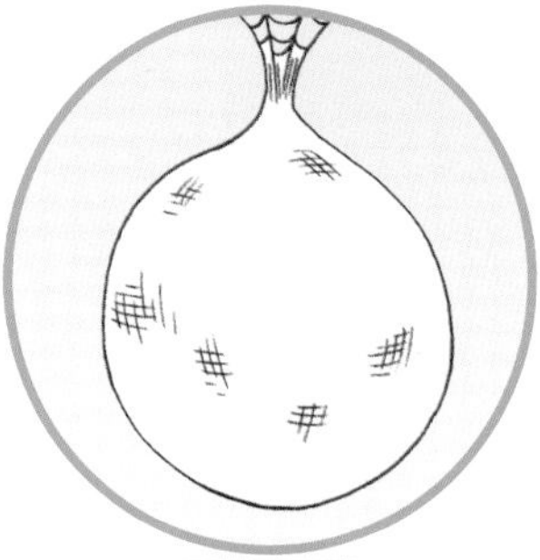

silk

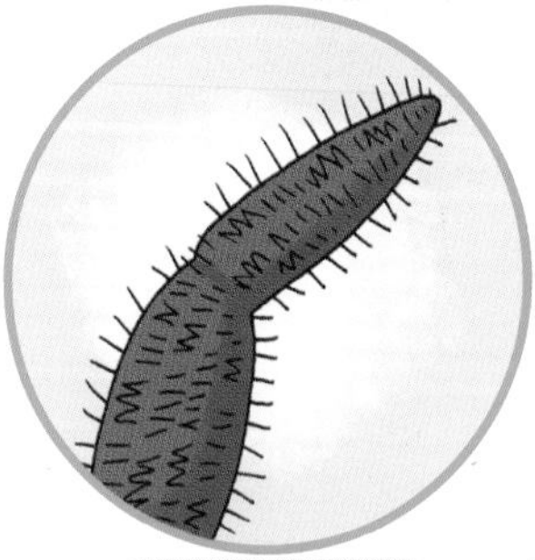

sticky

upside-down

web

1 Look and match

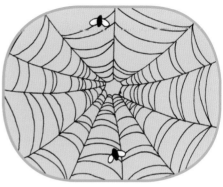

catch food

change colour

upside-down

climb

2 Listen and say

Collins

Published by Collins
An imprint of HarperCollins*Publishers*
Westerhill Road
Bishopbriggs
Glasgow
G64 2QT

HarperCollins*Publishers*
1st Floor, Watermarque Building
Ringsend Road
Dublin 4
Ireland

William Collins' dream of knowledge for all began with the publication of his first book in 1819.

A self-educated mill worker, he not only enriched millions of lives, but also founded a flourishing publishing house. Today, staying true to this spirit, Collins books are packed with inspiration, innovation and practical expertise. They place you at the centre of a world of possibility and give you exactly what you need to explore it.

© HarperCollins*Publishers* Limited 2020

10 9 8 7 6 5 4 3 2

ISBN 978-0-00-839788-3

Collins® and COBUILD® are registered trademarks of HarperCollins*Publishers* Limited

www.collins.co.uk/elt

Author: Julie Penn
Illustrator: Abdi (Beehive)
Series editor: Rebecca Adlard
Commissioning editor: Fiona Undrill
Publishing manager: Lisa Todd
Product managers: Jennifer Hall and Caroline Green
In-house editor: Alma Puts Keren
Project manager: Emily Hooton
Editor: Tessie Papadopoulou-Dalton
Proofreaders: Natalie Murray and Michael Lamb
Cover designer: Kevin Robbins
Typesetter: 2Hoots Publishing Services Ltd
Audio produced by id audio, London
Reading guide author: Emma Wilkinson
Production controller: Rachel Weaver
Printed and bound by: GPS Group, Slovenia

Download the audio for this book and a reading guide for parents and teachers at www.collins.co.uk/839788